JOURNEY TO
THE BRIGHT KINGDOM

JOURNEY TO THE BRIGHT KINGDOM

by Elizabeth Winthrop

illustrated by Charles Mikolaycak

Holiday House · New York

Text copyright © 1979 by Elizabeth Winthrop Mahony
Illustrations copyright © 1979 by Charles Mikolaycak
All rights reserved. Printed in the U.S.A.

Library of Congress Cataloging in Publication Data

Winthrop, Elizabeth.
    Journey to the bright kingdom.

    SUMMARY: The mice of Kakure-sato grant a blind woman
temporary sight during the journey she and her kind
daughter make to their magical underground kingdom.
    [1. Folklore—Japan. 2. Blind—Fiction.
3. Physically handicapped—Fiction. 4. Mice—Fiction]
I. Mikolaycak, Charles. II. Title.
PZ8.1.W752Jo   [398.2] [E]   78-23261
ISBN 0-8234-0357-2

For John, with thanks

This story is an adaptation of the well-known Japanese folktale, The Rolling Rice Cakes, which tells of a man who entered Kakure-sato, a mythical kingdom ruled by mice.

When this man went to his fields one day to gather firewood, he accidentally dropped his lunch into a hole. As he was leaning over to retrieve the rice cakes, he heard tiny singing voices. Overcome by curiosity, he tumbled down the hole to the rich world of Kakure-sato. The mice insisted he return home, and gave him a present of a very small bale of rice. The tiny bale turned out to be a magical gift because it stayed full to the top, no matter how much rice was taken from it.

I was first introduced to this story in the Manga, or Hokusai sketchbooks. Katsushika Hokusai (1760-1849) was a famous Japanese print-maker who drew landscapes, folktale characters, and many popular scenes in Japanese life.

ELIZABETH WINTHROP

JOURNEY TO
THE BRIGHT KINGDOM

ONCE THERE WAS a young man who lived with his wife in a small cottage by the side of the big brown river. Every morning, the man rose early and went down to the river to run the ferryboat back and forth from one side to the other. After her husband had left the house, the young woman took her pencil and her sketch pad and went out to the fields to draw. She loved the sky and the trees and the smell of the spring earth newly turned over by the farmer's plow. And everything that she saw and touched and smelled, she drew into her pictures. Gradually, news of her work spread throughout the countryside, and people came from all over to buy her drawings. "She has shown us things that we never noticed before," the people said to each other. And they were right, for this young woman had a remarkable gift for seeing everything around her from the smallest black beetle to the great blue sky.

SHE LOVED the buzzing of the bees in the late
spring when the clover was thick, and the songs
of the birds in the early morning, and the full
open sun hot on her back in the middle of
summer. Often, as she sat on her stool, bent
over her sketch pad, she would see out of the
corner of her eye the darting of a small gray

field mouse, sniffing along the furrows for a grain of wheat. "Come back," she would call as he bounded away. "Come talk to me of your kingdom." For ever since she was a child, she had heard the story of Kakure-sato, the magical kingdom where, day and night, the mice pounded on their bales of rice. "The mice have all the riches of the earth underground," her father used to tell her as she sat on his lap. "May I go there?" she would ask. And her father would smile and shrug his shoulders. "Only certain people are allowed to see Kakure-sato. The mice decide who it will be."

One day, the woman came home with a terrible ache in her head. The next morning when she woke up, the lines around the room were blurred. A week later, she could barely see the picture on her sketch pad. In one month, she had gone totally blind.

She and her husband traveled to one doctor after another. But when they examined her, they shook their heads sadly and looked at the floor. "There is no cure for this blindness," they said. And the young woman pressed her hands to her eyes to hold back the tears because, even when you are blind, you can still cry.

They returned home, and the husband went back to work on the ferryboat. Slowly, the woman learned to feel her way around the house, so that her husband's supper would be waiting on the table when he came home. And she learned to feel the stitches with her fingertips, so that the holes in his trousers were mended. And she tried to smile when he told

her about his day and the people who had taken rides across the brown river in his boat. "She has grown used to the blindness," he thought to himself as time went on. "She does not mind it so much anymore." But he did not know how she sat at the window when he was gone and listened to the birds singing and smelled the spring flowers and touched the raindrops on the windowsill. He never knew how much she cried when she was all alone.

One day, when her husband came home, his wife had a strange, secret smile on her face. He asked her what was making her smile but she turned away and would not answer. After that day, she was changed, and she did not sit by the window all the time waiting and listening. She went out often, feeling her way down the path to her neighbor's gate and then along the stone wall to where she could hear the stream bubbling over the rocks. The neighbors would look out and see her standing there with her head cocked, talking quietly to herself.

"She's finally gone mad with the blindness," the neighbor's wife said to her husband one night. "She sits on the rock and talks to the air. There is nobody there to hear her."

"Poor woman," the neighbor said, shaking his head.

One night, the blind woman took her husband's hand and laid it on her stomach. From inside, there came a flutter like the wings of a butterfly beating against a flower.

"In May the baby will come," she told him. "In my favorite month."

KIYO WAS BORN in May. When the little girl was laid beside her, the mother reached out and gently touched the baby's face with her fingertips, running her hands over the fine, smooth skin and the small bump of a nose.

"Is she pretty?" the wife asked her husband.

"She is beautiful."

"Tell me what she looks like."

"She has bright black eyes and a round face and a tiny pink mouth."

"Oh, I wish I could see her," the wife cried, pulling the baby close and rocking her. Her husband went out of the room quickly so that she could not hear him crying.

The baby grew fast and, every day, her mother would strap Kiyo on her back and take her out for a walk in the spring sun. And the mother would tell the baby what she was seeing.

"The cherry trees are all blossoming now. Look up, Kiyo, and see their pink blooms. There must be a robin sitting up in the branches because I can hear him singing. Do you see him?"

At first, the baby could only gurgle and laugh at the soft sound of her mother's voice. But as Kiyo grew older and began to understand what her mother was saying, she learned to look around her at the things her mother could no longer see.

One day, when they were sitting out under the trees and shelling the garden peas, Kiyo's mother told her about Kakure-sato. Kiyo listened to the story of the gray mice and their rich kingdom under the earth. "Tell me more," she cried in delight. So her mother told her that in Kakure-sato, the grass was the richest color of green and the air was clear and cool, like a morning in the mountains, and the streams were full of silver fish. "No one is unhappy in this magical kingdom," she said dreamily. "Nobody is tired or hurt or lonely or —" she stopped. "Or blind," she said quietly. And Kiyo looked into her mother's blank eyes and said nothing.

The years passed and soon Kiyo was old enough to walk to school by herself. She had a long way to go because their cottage was the farthest one out of the village, but she did not mind the walk because there was always so much to look at. Everything she saw she described to her mother.

Often, when Kiyo's father came home from work, he would find his wife and daughter deep in conversation, the little one's hands and face talking as fast as her voice. And the mother seemed to be listening with her whole body, as if somehow she could see just by hearing the words.

ONE AFTERNOON, Kiyo took a different path home from school. The forest trees grew thick above her head, and soon there were only small spots of light on the path. Just as she was about to go back, she saw what looked like an opening up ahead of her. She turned a corner in the path and came to a large field where the wind was blowing through the tops of the wheat stalks. She stood at the edge of the field, her eyes blinking in the sunlight that seemed strong after the dark forest.

"I will stop here and eat my last rice cake," she said as she walked down the rows of wheat looking for a place to sit. While she ate, she looked at the clear sky, at the sparrows diving and darting for the grains of wheat on the ground, at a black beetle laboring up and down the furrows of cracked, dry earth. It was late summer, and the sun felt warm. She leaned back and closed her eyes for a minute. When she opened them again, there was a small gray mouse eating up the last crumbs of her rice cake. He darted away when she sat up.

"There's some more," she called with a laugh. "Come back. I won't hurt you."

Then, to Kiyo's amazement, his tiny face reappeared over the edge of the furrow, his pink nose sniffing and twitching.

"Still hungry?" Kiyo asked softly. "Here, I will put the crumbs down on the ground near you."

And while he ate, she talked to him quietly.

"This is a beautiful field you live in. I have never been here before. I usually come home from school along the river but, since this is the first day of the new school year, I decided to find a different way to come home. I saw this path going off through the woods, and so I took it."

The mouse ate daintily, sitting up on his back legs. Every so often, he would stop and study her face as if he were listening to what she was saying. When he was finished, he cleaned his paws carefully and darted away after a quick nod of his gray head.

"Come see me again," she called after him as she stood up to leave. Then she ran home to tell her mother about the field and the gray mouse.

"I remember that field," her mother said softly. "I went there often to paint. It was there that I —" she stopped.

"That what, Mama?"

"I first felt the headaches. The time I went

blind." She was silent for a minute. "So you have met the mice. They were always shy with me."

"Just one mouse," Kiyo said. "But I felt as if he were listening to me. I am going to come home that way again tomorrow."

Every afternoon from then on, Kiyo came home through the field. She was always sure to save one rice cake from her lunch to feed to the mice. Soon, her mother began making extra cakes because so many mice were waiting for Kiyo in the afternoons.

Kiyo sat on her rock surrounded by a circle of friends, all busy eating and sniffing and skipping around her feet. And as they ate, she talked to them about her mother and father and her days at school. After a while, she began to recognize some of them. There was the old mouse who walked very stiffly. The others were polite to him and allowed him to eat first. There was a family of three. The father often seemed exhausted by his young son who scampered about endlessly, knocking into other older mice and playing tag with the younger ones. He came closer to Kiyo than the others and tried to catch her attention with his somersaults and his running games. His mother was shy, and she hung back, waiting for her husband to bring her some crumbs. There were two old females who chattered and fussed over their food, rolling each crumb delicately around in their paws before they popped it into their mouths. Kiyo told her mother about each of them, and together they laughed over their new friends, the mice.

"Ask them about Kakure-sato," her mother urged Kiyo.

"You are putting foolish ideas in the girl's head," her husband said. "There is no such place."

"Ask them," the mother said again to her daughter.

So the next afternoon, when the mice were once again gathered at her feet, Kiyo asked them about their magical kingdom. "It was very strange," she told her mother that night. "I am sure they understood me. Suddenly, they stopped what they were doing and stared at me."

"Watch where they go when they leave you," her mother said. "Maybe you can follow them."

But every afternoon, when Kiyo stood up to leave, the mice darted away so quickly that she could not follow them with her eyes. One minute they were there, and the next minute they were gone.

Summer turned to fall, and the afternoon wind grew cool. The sun set a little earlier every day, and Kiyo could not sit and talk for long because she had to be home before dark.

"There are not as many mice who come to eat my cakes," Kiyo said to her father one November afternoon.

"They are busy now, gathering food for the winter," her father explained. "Soon they will go underground until the spring comes. It will be too cold for you to stop and talk. You must hurry home with the wood for your mother's fire."

THE FIRST SNOW fell in early December and, when Kiyo came through the field collecting wood, no mice popped up to greet her. She called out once or twice from her place by the rock but the only thing moving was a black crow high in the gray sky. She crumbled up her rice cake on the crusty snow and hurried home with the wood, for the day was cold, and she knew her mother would be waiting.

Her mother was sitting in a chair by the window.

"It is too cold to sit there, Mama," Kiyo said. "Come here and I will build the fire."

"Is the snow deep?" asked her mother.

"Only a few inches," Kiyo answered.

"There is more coming," said her mother, pulling her shawl close around her. "I can smell it in the air."

"The sky is very gray. But come feel how warm it is over here," Kiyo said, taking her mother's hand and leading her away from the window. When she had settled her mother by the fire, Kiyo set about fixing dinner, talking brightly about the way the snow had changed the look of everything. But for once, her mother was silent and did not ask her usual questions. When Kiyo's father got home, he saw immediately that something was wrong.

"Do you feel all right?" he asked his wife.

"It is nothing," she said, trying to smile. "Just the winter coming on. It always makes me sad."

Kiyo saw her father watching his wife that evening with a worried expression on his face. She sat silently by the fire and, when Kiyo tried to get her to eat her dinner, she said she wasn't hungry.

It did snow more that night just as Kiyo's mother had said it would. The next afternoon, Kiyo came home by the road because the path through the woods had disappeared under the snowdrifts. It was dark by the time she arrived and, as the days went by, she grew used to seeing her mother's drawn face at the window in the same place she had left her in the morning.

"Oh, Mama, it's so dark in here," she said as she opened the door. "You haven't lit the candles."

"I don't need candles," her mother said softly. As she turned her head away, Kiyo saw the tears rolling down her cheeks.

"Mama, what is it?" the little girl cried. "Can't I do something for you?"

But her mother just shook her head and waved her away.

Kiyo's father grew more and more worried about his wife. Sometimes, when he got home from work, she was already in bed, her body stiff, her blank eyes staring up at the ceiling. When he questioned her, she would refuse to answer. He and Kiyo spoke about it in whispers every night as they sat by the fire. Finally, they decided that she should see the doctor, even though the trip would take two days because of the deep snow. When they let her know their decision, she agreed to go although she told

them it was useless. "No doctor will cure me of this disease," she said. "Unless he can give me back my eyes."

It turned out that she was right. When they returned from the journey, Kiyo was waiting for them, and she could see the disappointment in her father's eyes.

"There is nothing physically wrong with her," he told Kiyo late that night after her mother had gone to bed. "She has just given up. She told the doctor that if she could never see again, she did not want to go on living."

Kiyo began to try even harder to spark her mother's interest. The next afternoon, when Kiyo got home to the dark house, she brought her mother a branch from an evergreen tree and a pine cone with the snow still caught in its crevices.

"The stream is completely covered with ice, Mama, and I could walk across it instead of taking the bridge. Uncle Yaki says this is the worst winter we have ever had. He has been feeding the birds every afternoon because the snow is too deep for them to find food. I wonder how my mice are doing."

"Have you been to the field?" her mother asked, turning the pine cone over in her fingers.

"The snow is too deep in the woods. I can't find the path."

"They are safe in their kingdom," her mother said dreamily. She did not say anything more but Kiyo noticed that she kept the pine cone close by her bed, and she reached out often during the evening to touch it.

SLOWLY, the first signs of spring appeared. The
dawn came earlier than before, and the sun
began to melt the snow.

"The snow is almost gone, Mama," Kiyo said
one afternoon. "Tomorrow, I will come home
through the field."

Her mother nodded. She was sitting in a chair
by the window for the first time in months.

"I think I hear a robin," she said quietly.
"Listen." Kiyo stood by her, and they listened for
a minute.

"You're right, Mama," Kiyo said. "There is a
robin in the tree at the end of the garden."
Once again, she was amazed at how much her
mother knew about the world around her
without being able to see it.

"I want to see him," the blind woman said,
her voice trembling with anger. There was a
silence between them. "Go away, child. Leave
me alone. I am not myself today."

So Kiyo went outside to wait for her father.

The next day, Kiyo found her old path through the woods. The air was cold but everywhere she looked, there was the promise of spring. In the stream bed, the bright-green shoots of the skunk cabbage stood up from the dark earth. The trees were feathery with the very first buds. When she came near to the field, she broke into a run. Her rock was still there, moist and shining from the morning's melting. She stood on top of it and called for the mice. After what seemed like ages, one small gray head popped up at her feet.

"Oh," Kiyo cried. "You are still here. Here is your rice cake," she said, crumbling it up for him. He crept up the side of the rock and nibbled at her feet, his eyes watching her carefully.

"How was your winter?" she asked. "It must have been terrible out here with all that snow. We had a bad time, too."

He stopped eating and looked up at her.

"It's my mother," she said softly. "She has been sad all winter. She says if she can never see again, she doesn't want to live anymore." And Kiyo went on to tell him the whole story. The mouse sat still, listening intently, the last crumbs of the cake untouched on the ground.

"There hasn't been anyone else to tell," Kiyo said shyly. "I didn't mean to keep you so long."

But the mouse didn't move. He opened his mouth and said something which she couldn't hear, so she leaned over and put her ear right next to his face.

"Bring her here," the mouse squeaked.

"Oh, Mama could never make it all the way here. It would be impossible," Kiyo cried but even as she said it, she was thinking that they might be able to lead her along the footpath of the river if her father helped her.

"Bring her here," the mouse said again. "We will be waiting." And with that, he hopped away and was soon lost from sight.

During dinner that night, Kiyo was very quiet. Even her mother noticed it.

"Kiyo, did you come home through the field today?" she asked.

"Yes, Mama."

"Well, aren't you going to tell me about it?"

"One mouse came to eat my rice cake. He looked very thin. The winter must have been bad for them."

Her mother asked no more questions. She went to bed early. "What's wrong with you, Kiyo?" her father said that evening. "You seem distracted today."

"It's the mouse I saw, Papa. I told him about Mama and how worried we both have been, and he spoke to me. No, really," she cried when she saw the doubt on his face. "He told me to take Mama to the field. He said they would be waiting."

"Kiyo, that's impossible. She could never make it that far. And what good would it do?" He reached out to pat her shoulder. "Your mother loves the tales of your mice. But you must not get carried away with them. Go to bed now."

Kiyo tried to say something more, but he waved her away.

THE NEXT DAY, when Kiyo stopped at her rock, four mice came up to her feet, led by the one who had spoken to her the day before.

"You did not bring her," the leader said sternly.

Kiyo shook her head. "My father says it is too far. She will never make it. He says it would do her no good."

At that, the four mice formed a circle and talked among themselves. Kiyo sat on the rock, straining to hear what they were saying.

After what seemed like a long time, the leader held up his paw and turned back to Kiyo. "You have been generous with your rice cakes," he said. "We would like to help you now. We are the mice of Kakure-sato. If you bring your mother to us, we will take you both there for one visit. In our magical kingdom under the ground, nobody is deaf or mute or crippled or blind. While she is there, she will be able to see."

Kiyo could not believe her ears. In her

excitement, she jumped up quickly, and the mice scattered to avoid being trampled.

"Oh, I'm sorry I scared you. I must rush home now to tell my father. I will bring her tomorrow, no matter what."

One of the mice motioned to her to bend down again. Kiyo recognized him as the old one for whom the others had always shown such great respect.

"You will not have another chance," he said. "This is a dangerous decision for us to make. There are many evil people who want to get to Kakure-sato and rob us of our riches. After tomorrow, you will not see us again."

But still her father would not hear of it. "My child, you have let your imagination run away with you. There is no such place as Kakure-sato. It only exists in the tales that old men tell to their grandchildren."

No matter how much Kiyo pleaded with him, she could not change his mind.

The next day, after her father left for work, Kiyo took a cup of tea into her mother's room.

"Is that you, Kiyo?" her mother said. "I thought you had already left for school."

"I'm not going to school today, Mama," Kiyo said softly. "Drink your tea, and I will put on your shoes. We are going on a trip."

Her mother looked puzzled. "What do you mean?"

"The mice spoke to me yesterday, Mama. I told them about the winter, how sad you have been. They want me to take you to the field. They want to take us down to Kakure-sato."

Her mother sighed. "Don't be foolish, Kiyo. There is no such place."

"But you have always told me about it," Kiyo cried. "I thought you believed in their magical kingdom. You were the one who told me how green the grass grows there and how clear the water is and how you can hear the birds singing even though you are underground."

Her mother reached out to touch her daughter's face. "Don't be disappointed in me, Kiyo. I do still believe in Kakure-sato the way I believe in the robin even though I can no longer see him. But you must understand that a blind person lives in another world. Her dreams cannot always be trusted."

"The mice say that while you are there, you will be able to see again. We can only go this one time, and I promised them I would bring you today."

There was a silence. Kiyo's mother was sitting up very straight in bed, and there was a frown on her face.

"How far is your field?" she asked. "I cannot even remember."

"Not too far, Mama. We could make it there and be home by dark. I could lead you along the river path," Kiyo said.

"And I would be able to see again?"

"Yes, Mama, but just for the time we are there."

Her mother leaned over and felt along the floor for her shoes. "Then we will go," she said. "We will go see your friends, the mice. Here, give me your hand."

THERE WERE TIMES during the trip that Kiyo
thought they would never make it. Her mother
was weak from having stayed inside all winter.
She stumbled despite Kiyo's warnings and
guiding hands, and they had to stop often so she
could rest.

"I don't think I can make it, Kiyo," her mother
cried when they stopped for the third time. "I'm
just too weak."

Kiyo felt suddenly scared. They were only
halfway to the field, and her mother's face
looked gray and drawn. She knew how angry
her father would be if he found out what she
had done. And she wasn't sure that if they ever
reached the field, she would be able to get her
mother home again.

"Kiyo, are you there?" her mother asked,
reaching out her hands.

"Yes, I'm here," she answered quickly. "Do
you feel well enough to go on now? The mice
are waiting for us. Finally, you will see Kakure-
sato, Mama."

Her mother touched her blank open eyes. She
took a deep breath and stood up again. "Let's
go," she said with a smile.

The four mice were waiting for them at the edge of the field.

Kiyo waved when she saw the gray figures standing together on a rock.

"You came," the leader said. "I was sure you would."

"We have been waiting a long time," said another of the mice.

"It must have been a long trip for you both," said the oldest mouse.

"It has been long," Kiyo's mother said quietly. "But it was worth it."

"Come with us," the leader said, turning and hopping off towards the middle of the field.

After a short distance, he stopped and signaled to his companions. They lined up behind Kiyo and her mother. Kiyo was directed to take hold of the leader's tail, and her mother put her hands on Kiyo's shoulders. They closed their eyes. Soon, they felt the ground moving under them, and they began to roll over and over as if they were falling down a hole. When they stopped, Kiyo opened her eyes. She saw before her a huge crowd of mice sitting quietly watching them. Behind the mice, there were great mountains of rice. Beyond that, she saw a door that led into a larger room where she could hear the sound of falling water and birds singing. Kiyo glanced at her mother, who was standing quietly beside her.

"I can see you, Kiyo," she said softly, her eyes shining with tears. "We are finally here, and I can see my own daughter's face." Kiyo put her

arms around her mother, and they held each other close for a long time. Around them, the mice sat in hushed silence, waiting.

"Look around you, Mama," Kiyo said softly. "You must not waste a minute of your time."

"I am looking," her mother answered with a laugh. "And I can see it all." Her eyes were open, and the blank look was gone from them. For the first time, Kiyo saw her mother the way she used to be. Her face was alive, her eyes drinking in every color, every movement, every shadow and shaft of light.

"Hello, Kiyo," called a voice from the middle of the crowd. "We missed your rice cakes over the winter."

"My wife and I used to visit with you every afternoon," said a mouse in the front row. "You remember our son?"

"Here I am," cried the tiny mouse right under her feet.

"Oh, yes," Kiyo said. "The one who does the somersaults."

The little mouse was so pleased that he did a somersault right then and there.

By now, all the mice were calling to her, waving their tails for attention. She looked around helplessly, trying to answer each one. After a while, the leader lifted up his paws to quiet them.

"We don't have much time," he said. "And we must show our friends everything. Come along, Kiyo."

The crowd parted, and Kiyo and her mother walked through behind the leader. Kiyo stopped

once or twice to introduce her mother to some of the mice she recognized from their afternoon talks.

"You see, she knows the difference between us," one mouse squeaked to a friend. "Most humans think we all look alike."

The mouse in front led them down a tunnel, and the other mice followed squeaking with excitement. They passed a mountain of sparkling rocks and streams of clear, running water. Silver fish darted in and out among the green plants that waved back and forth in the current. Overhead, the trees were filled with singing birds, and the grass underneath their feet shone like blades of emerald. Even though they were underground, the air was fresh and smelled of the first spring flowers.

"This is our kingdom," said the mouse who was walking beside Kiyo. "We have the riches of the earth here."

"We wanted you to see it," said another mouse who was riding on her shoulder.

"And then when we heard about your mother, we knew how much it would mean to her to visit us," the leader explained. "We remember when she used to come paint in our field."

"Kiyo, look," the blind woman cried as she knelt down on the grass. "Lilies of the valley. I thought I smelled them when we first turned the corner. Did you see the nest the doves built in the cherry tree? I could hear them calling out to each other. And the willow trees," she sighed, sitting back on her heels. She reached up to touch their leaves. "Their leaves are so delicate in the beginning. I had forgotten how bright their first yellow is."

Kiyo smiled happily. The long trip had been worth it, just to see such a look of pleasure on her mother's face.

The mice led them to a place under the trees where a great feast had been laid out. They ate heartily, complimenting the mice on the delicate taste of each tiny dish. When they had finished, the leader signaled to two mice who came forward carrying a very small bale of rice.

"We would like to give you this present," the leader said solemnly. "May you eat it in good health."

Kiyo accepted the present just as solemnly, although she wondered how they would ever be able to divide this tiny portion of rice among three people.

Then the leader turned to Kiyo's mother. "You know that you will be blind again once you leave Kakure-sato. Our magic has no power in the world above. We brought you here because we wanted to show you again how beautiful the world can be. But you are a different person from the woman we used to watch painting in the fields. Back then, you saw only with your eyes. Today, you saw Kakure-sato with your ears and your fingers and your nose."

Kiyo's mother looked down at the ground. "I understand what you are saying to me." A look passed between the mouse and the blind woman that startled Kiyo. "They look as if they are speaking some special language," she

thought. "As if they have met somewhere before."

"You have given me the best present of all," said the woman. "At last, I have been able to see my daughter's face. I will carry the picture of her around inside my head for the rest of my life."

"And now, it is time for you to go. It will soon be dark up above, and you have a long way to travel." He led them to the entrance of another tunnel. "Take one more look," he said to the mother. "It will be your last."

She stood for a long silent minute, her eyes wide and staring. There was not a sound in the room. They all knew what this meant to her. "All right," she whispered. "I am ready." Then she and Kiyo held hands and closed their eyes. "Good-bye," they called. "Thank you." There was a rush of air and that same sensation of rolling over and over. When they stopped moving, they were standing alone in the middle of the field. The sun was low in the sky, and the air felt cool.

"We must hurry, Mama," Kiyo said, taking her mother's hand. "Father will be home soon."

But her mother did not move and, when Kiyo glanced up at her face, she could see the tears rolling down her mother's cheeks. "Oh, Mama," Kiyo cried, hugging her.

"It's all right," said her mother. "I just couldn't help myself at first. It was so hard to be back in this black world all over again. But it's all right now." She smiled. "Now, when I hear your voice, I can see your face in front of me. As long as I can see you, I am not truly blind."

THEY NEVER TOLD Kiyo's father about their trip.
"He wouldn't believe us," they decided. He was
delighted with the change in his wife. When he
got home, she was often out in the front yard
waiting for him, her body tuned to the sounds
and smells of the evening. That spring, for the
first time since she had gone blind, she insisted
on planting their garden herself, and she tended
it just as carefully as she had in the old days. "I
can feel the plants growing," she told her

husband with a laugh. She took long walks by herself during the day and, when her husband cautioned her about going too far, she just waved away his warnings. "I can always smell my way home," she explained.

"What has happened to her?" he asked Kiyo. "It's almost as if she can see."

Kiyo just smiled and said nothing.

Although Kiyo went back to the field often, she never saw the mice again.

"Why don't they come back?" she asked her mother sadly. "Do you think they are angry with me?"

"No, Kiyo. But I don't think you will ever see them again. Now that we have been to Kakure-sato, we could become dangerous to them. If anybody learned of our adventure, they might try to follow us to the mice, and discover their kingdom. At least, we will always have their bale of rice."

For soon after they had gotten home that evening, Kiyo and her mother had discovered that their tiny bale of rice was very special. No matter how many times they scooped out a spoonful to cook for their dinner, the bale remained full to the top. "It's magic," Kiyo had exclaimed. "One of the riches of their kingdom," her mother had answered softly.

And even when she had grown old, and Kiyo's children were the ones who led her down to the orchard to hear the first robins singing in the spring, the blind woman could still see from inside her dark world the bright kingdom of Kakure-sato.

S

Journey to the bright kingdom

DISCARD

Rockingham Public Library
Harrisonburg, Virginia   22801